SO-BYB-436

E
MCD

McDonald, Megan.

Beezy.

$14.99

DATE			
		REMOVED	

BEEZY

stories by Megan McDonald

illustrated by Nancy Poydar

Orchard Books   New York

Orchard Books, 95 Madison Avenue, New York, NY 10016

Manufactured in the United States of America
Printed by Barton Press, Inc. Bound by Horowitz/Rae
The text of this book is set in 20 point Stempel Garamond.
The illustrations are gouache paintings reproduced in full color.

10 9 8 7 6 5 4 3 2 1

Library of Congress Cataloging-in-Publication Data
McDonald, Megan.
Beezy / stories by Megan McDonald ; illustrated by Nancy Poydar.
p. cm. "A Richard Jackson book."
Summary: Beezy and her best friend Merlin, who live in Florida,
wait out a hurricane, find a dog, and make friends with a
circus performer.
ISBN 0-531-30046-3.—ISBN 0-531-33046-X (lib. bdg.)
[1. Friendship—Fiction. 2. Florida—Fiction.]
I. Poydar, Nancy, ill. II. Title.
PZ7.M478419Be   1997   [E]—dc21   96-53866

For Louise, Annie,
and Eliza

—M.M.

Contents

Eye of the Storm   7

Funnybone   23

Sarafina Zippy   33

Eye of the Storm

Wind blew.

Wind rattled the windows
of the old house
where Beezy lived with Gran.

"A real Florida storm," said Gran.

"Maybe a hurricane."

Knock knock.

"Someone is at the door,"

said Beezy.

"Just the wind," Gran said.

"Merlin!" said Beezy.

"We thought you were the wind."

Merlin was wet.

"I ran all the way

from my house," Merlin said.

"I ran six blocks to tell you

there might be a hurricane.

Right here in Soda Springs!"

"Your best friend is
out in the rain, Beezy," Gran said.
"Let him in."
Merlin dripped a puddle on the floor.
He dripped a puddle on the chair.
"Get Merlin a towel, Beezy."
Knock knock knock.

"Who could that be?" Gran asked.

"Just the rain," said Beezy.

"Gumm!" Gran said.

"We thought you
were the rain."

"I closed up shop," said Mr. Gumm.
"I ran three blocks to tell you
there might be a hurricane.
Right here in Soda Springs!"
"Gran," said Beezy.
"Your best friend is
out in the rain."
"I have candles," Mr. Gumm said.
"In case the lights go out."
"Scary," said Merlin.
"Spooky," said Beezy.
The lights blinked.
Off. On. Off. On.

The house went dark.

Gran lit the candles.

The candles made spooky shadows.

"Now what?" Beezy asked.

"We wait out the storm," Gran said.

"You mean hurricane," said Merlin.

"We can tell stories,"
Mr. Gumm said.

"Ghost stories!" said Beezy.

"Hurricane stories!" Merlin cried.

Mr. Gumm began:

"When I was just a boy

and your gran was just a girl—"

"You knew Gran way back then?"

Beezy asked.

"I knew your gran
back in the days
when stones were soft."
"Wow," said Merlin.
"Yes, sir. Hurricane Jane. 1942.
She blew up the coast
from the Florida Keys."

"Remember the red sky?"
Gran asked.

"Sunset red as a beet,"
Mr. Gumm said.

"Winds faster than a car can drive."

"Wow," said Beezy.

"She could snap trees in half.
Lifted the roof right off the house!
We hid in the dark
and ate peanut butter crackers,"
said Mr. Gumm.
"Sang songs till it got quiet,"
Gran said.

"Eye of the storm," said Mr. Gumm.
"Until a wall of water
rolled down the street."
"Dropped a washing machine
right in the front yard," Gran said.
"Wow," said Merlin.

Beezy and Merlin
and Gran and Mr. Gumm
ate peanut butter crackers,
sang songs, and told stories
till the lights came on.
"The storm is over," Gran said.

"Let's go look outside," said Merlin.

"I don't see any washing machines," said Beezy.

"Oh, well," Merlin said. "Maybe we will have another hurricane tomorrow."

Funnybone

Beezy made a wish.

She wished for a dog.

One day she found a dog

in the alley.

She gave him an old bone.

A funny-looking bone.

He followed her.

To school.

To Mr. Gumm's store.

To the baseball park.

Home.

Beezy named him

Funnybone.

"Some other girl might love
this dog," said Gran.

Funnybone looked at Gran
with sad eyes.
His ears drooped.
His tail flopped.
He jumped on Gran
and licked her face all over.
Gran made a sign:

FOUND
Small cute dog.
Face half brown.
Half white.
One blue eye.
One brown eye

Mr. Gumm let Gran hang the sign
in his store window.
Beezy and Merlin walked past
the sign.
One time. Two times.
Three times in one day.
"What if someone calls?
What if someone comes?

Then Funnybone will not be
my dog."
"We could take the sign down,"
Merlin said.
"Mr. Gumm would see us,"
said Beezy.
"We could hide Funnybone,"
Merlin said.
"Gran would find him," said Beezy.

She waited.

And waited.

And wished.

A week went by.

Two weeks.

Three weeks.

No one called!

No one came!

Funnybone followed Beezy.

To school.

To Mr. Gumm's store.

To the baseball park.

Home.

"Jump," said Beezy.
Funnybone jumped.
Beezy and Funnybone
jumped and chased
dandelion seeds
in the air.

29

"Stay," said Beezy.

She climbed up in her tree house.

Funnybone stayed.

"Good dog."

Beezy climbed down.

"Roll over," said Beezy.
Funnybone rolled over
in the grass.
Funnybone and Beezy
rolled down
the grassy hill.
Beezy and Funnybone.
Funnybone and Beezy.
"You're mine,"
said Beezy.

Sarafina Zippy

Merlin had a new card trick
for Beezy.

"Think of a card," Merlin said.

"King of hearts," said a voice
from behind the bushes.

"Oh, no," Beezy said to Merlin.

"That new girl.

They say she has a tattoo.

They say she is from the circus."

"Cool," said Merlin.

The new girl stepped out

from behind the bushes.

She was short.

She wore an alligator-tooth necklace.

"Maybe she's a midget,"

Beezy said to Merlin.

The new girl rode her unicycle

up the sidewalk.

"Show-off," said Beezy to Merlin.

"Pick a card," Merlin told

the new girl.

The girl pulled a card from the deck.

"King of hearts!" the new girl said.

"How did you do that?"

"Magic," said Merlin.

The girl pulled out a dime

from behind her ear.

She gave the dime to Merlin.

"Wow," Merlin said.

"How did you do that?"

"Magic," said the girl.

"I'm Merlin," said Merlin.

"This is Beezy."

"I'm Sarafina Zippy,"

the new girl said.

"Is that a circus name?"
Merlin asked.

"Beezy said you are a midget."

"I did not," said Beezy.

"I am not a midget,"
Sarafina Zippy said.

"But I know a fat lady
and a lion tamer.
My mom and dad are
the Flying Zippys.
In the Pickle Circus."
"Are you an acrobat too?"
asked Merlin.

Sarafina Zippy
rode her unicycle
backwards.

She did double flips
down the sidewalk.

"Double cool,"
Merlin said.
"Let's play checkers,
Merlin," said Beezy.

"Only two can play that,"
Merlin said.
"And you always get to be black."
"You like being red," said Beezy.
"My whole life,
as long as I have known you,
you have liked being red."

"Wow," Sarafina said.

"You knew Merlin your whole life?"

"Ever since I was two," said Beezy.

"Except for one week

when I was mad at him."

"The circus moves a lot,"
Sarafina told them.

"That's why we came to Florida.
The circus is here for the winter.
Maybe the summer too."

"Neat," said Merlin.

"Let's play Double Dutch,"
said Sarafina.

"Soupbone, funnybone,

Sweet potato pie . . ."

"Funnybone!" said Beezy.

"That's my dog's name."

Funnybone ran out
of the house.

He sniffed Sarafina's shoe.
He licked Sarafina's face.
Funnybone jumped rope too.
"He likes you," said Beezy.
Sarafina had a dog treat
in her pocket.

"I know how to make
this dog bone disappear."
"You do?" asked Merlin.
"You do?" asked Beezy.
"Ka-zam. When I open my hand,
the bone will be gone."
She opened her fist.
Funnybone snapped up the bone.
Merlin laughed.
Beezy laughed.
Funnybone licked his lips.
"Now what can we do?" Merlin asked.
"Let's look for gold," Sarafina said.

"And a lost shipwreck," said Beezy.

"I'll be Peg Leg Pete," Merlin said.

"Can Funnybone come too?" asked Beezy.

"Pirates can have dogs," Sarafina said.

"Let's go," said Beezy.